The Time Swiper

T.R. Ross

TRRoss

/Cincinnati, OH

Edited by James Daniel Ross
Interior Design by Tracy Renée Ross

Published by TriMoon Eclipse,
An imprint of Winter Wolf Publications, LLC

ISBN: 978-1-945039-25-6 (paperback)

Dedicated to my Purza

It has been quite a while since you passed, but I think of you every day. You were like a little ray of sunshine that is no longer there, and that part of me will remain dark until I see you again. I love you. I hope that, in the end, you felt my arms around you and heard my voice telling you that I was right there. I hope there really is a bridge and that you will be waiting on it for me on the other side of that rainbow.

~ Ma

T. R. Ross

Chapter 1

Within the sanctuary of my boy's arms, I sat and looked contentedly out over the room through half-closed eyes. A happy fire danced within the fireplace, and the entire family had stopped their busy day to all sit together and watch the moving picture across the large screen that dominated one side of the room, a screen they called a television. Around it, the place was decorated with brightly colored baubles, tinkling bells, and flickering multi-hued lights. Dad had brought a tree from the outside into the house and it stood sentinel in one corner of the room, looming over all. It was festooned with the most colorful of the baubles, a rope of shimmering tinsel, an artfully placed array of lights... and at the very top was the biggest and brightest light of them all: a winged figure that shone like a beacon of hope to all who looked upon it.

Wasp fairies were drawn to the lights the same way moths were. It was a battle to keep them all away from the tree, their tiny, lithe forms tumbling here and there among the branches. But Odin and I succeeded with minimal aggravation to Ma and Dad who thought that we just wanted to play in the tree. I didn't understand this rationale, but Odin explained that they simply didn't understand that we were trying to help. Not for the first time, I wished Ma and Dad could understand cat-speak. It would make life immensely easier.

However, above all of those things, the room was warm and cozy. The scent of my boy was all around me, as well as the aroma of something delicious baking in the oven. I felt safe and loved, not just by Sam, but by everyone in the family. Sam's three brothers sat around us on the sofa, and his four sisters took up the other sofa nearby. Ma and Dad sat together on the smaller loveseat, leaning against one another and holding hands. Between them was Odin.

A flood of additional security washed over me as I thought about the sleek silver-gray cat. In the weeks since I had first arrived, he had proven to me time and time again that I was important not just to the humans that made up this family, but to him. With Odin by my side, I felt stronger than I ever did alone, and he was my best friend.

Odin turned his head in my direction. His single golden eye took note of my location, the socket where the other eye should have been puckered and closed shut. He then turned away to complete his surveillance. It was his way, always knowing where each and every person was in the house. Protecting us all was his responsibility, and he took that very seriously.

The moving picture on the television ended and the family rose from their seats. As always, Sam's three brothers began to bicker among themselves. Sam and I continued to quietly sit, his hand softly stroking my long fur. It wasn't until Ma called everyone into the kitchen to partake of the chocolate chip cookies she had baked before my boy gently lifted me from his lap. He kissed me atop my head before letting me go to rush into the kitchen for his own share of the warm goodness Ma offered.

I proceeded to settle down upon the spot on the sofa that Sam had vacated. It was still warm, and suffused with his scent. Odin leapt up beside me, and if cats could smile, I know he would have done so by the twinkle in his eye as he touched his nose to mine in greeting. The big tom then settled himself beside me. "You look happy."

I thought about it for a moment and an image came to my mind... about another place, another boy, another life. *From his place in the bed, he held me in his arms, his blue eyes looking at me with loving devotion. But they were tired eyes, eyes that spoke of the battle he fought every day. Remembering the feel of his kisses, I reached up and licked him with my rough tongue. For just a moment, his eyes brightened with joy and the sweet sound of his giggles filled my ears and made my heart swell. Even without his blond hair, I knew him. I knew him by his scent beneath the cloying medicinal stench, by the sound of his voice even though it was so soft I could sometimes barely hear it, and by the feel of his love that had only grown bigger and stronger day after day after day.*

I lurched up from my place beside Odin, startling us both. Upon trembling legs, I stretched, arching my back and my tail to not only get myself moving, but to dislodge a memory that brought so much pain and fear.

Odin rose as well, his tail sweeping back and forth behind him in worry. "Freya, what is it?"

As the memory of the other boy faded from my mind, I looked at my friend and didn't know what to say. Yes, I was happy. I was very happy, and for some reason, that scared me. But I didn't want to say that. Odin wouldn't understand. How could he?

"It's nothing." I waved my tail and approached to rub my side against his in an expression of affection. "I believe bedtime is near, and you know how strict Ma can be about that."

Odin let his concern drop and he huffed in agreement with my statement. "Indeed."

The cats strolled into the kitchen just as everyone was finishing up with their cookies. The children put their plates in the sink while Ma put the leftovers in a storage container. Dad pinned me with a curious look. "Doesn't Freya look like she's getting bigger?"

Everyone stopped what they were doing to come and look at me. I just stood there, tail in the air and said, "Mrow?"

Ma came around the kitchen island and regarded me with a smile. She spoke in the singsong voice I had come to know and love. "Hey there, pretty girl." She proceeded to pick me up and hold me tenderly in her arms. "Aww, I guess she's getting a little round about the middle, but nothing to worry about. We will just monitor her food intake a bit."

All the children patted my head as they passed Ma and I on their way out of the kitchen. I basked in the glow of their affection, and when Ma put me back down, I twined myself about her legs. She smiled again. "You are such a good girl, Freya. I'm so glad we have you."

Chapter 2

Odin and I laid together on Sam's bed, the navy-blue comforter bundled like a nest all around us. Odin's side rose and fell with his breaths. They were slow and even, telling me he was deeply sleeping, and I was pleased to be there beside him. During sleep we are at our most vulnerable, and as such, only those we trust the most should be there with us. I am honored to hold this place in Odin's heart and mind.

I heard the front door open and close and I raised my head with a small, growl deep in my throat. Feeling the tension and hearing the growl, Odin awoke and raised his own head. "What is it?" he asked.

I cocked my head. "It's not time for anyone to be home from school or work."

Together we rose from our places and slunk out of the bedroom. We silently moved through the hallway and then down the stairs, smelling the scent of the outside that had recently come in when the door was opened. Halfway down we also smelled something new.

We both stopped and looked at the rectangular carrier set in the middle of the floor. It was the same one I arrived here in, one of the two used to transport both me and Odin to wherever Ma and Dad needed us to go. We could smell something new within, and it was feline.

A sense of protectiveness came over me, but I stifled the growl that struggled to be released. This was *my* territory... *my* house! These were *my* people, and the food here was mine! But when I looked back on the day I first arrived here, Odin had never growled at me. He had never made me feel unwelcome. He had opened this place up to me and shared everything. The least I could do was strive to be the same.

No matter how hard that might be.

I turned to look at Odin. He was the epitome of calm, his eye trained on the carrier. But when he noticed me watching, he butted me with his head.

"It looks like Ma has brought someone new home," he said nonchalantly.

A thought struck me and I asked, "Has she done this before?"

"Well, yes. Many times, especially in the old house."

I was aware that Ma and her four children and Dad and his four children had once lived in different homes. But when Ma and Dad got married, they had purchased this old house and moved everyone in. Odin had come with Ma, but all of Dad's children seemed to love him as though he was their cat too.

Odin tensed and his gaze was piercing as he looked at me. "But you are the only cat that has stayed with us. The others went to new homes after awhile."

This statement bid me pause, and it seemed to do the same for him. For a brief moment his gaze was speculative, but then, as though he'd come up with an answer to a question lurking in his mind, he relaxed. "It must be because you are special."

I just stayed there for another moment, taking in his statement. The icy grip of fear I'd felt from the other day intruded upon my thoughts and I was frozen in place, wondering... wondering...

"Come, we should greet the newcomer. She is afraid," said Odin.

And suddenly I could sense it too. The other cat was afraid, just like I had been when I first came here. Odin and I continued down the stairs, and once we reached the bottom, I could smell the familiar scent I hated so much, the scent of the place where I had been before coming here. It was strong, and pervasive, almost covering up another scent I picked up.

The cat was female.

I didn't realize I'd stopped until I noticed that Odin had left my side and was already crouched before the enclosed space. A growl could be heard emanating from within, one that bordered on panic.

Feeling more than a little insecure, I slowly approached. What if the new cat became Odin's best friend instead of me? What if he decided to replace me? A feeling of loneliness swept over me and I was sad. In the short time I'd lived here, I'd come to value the friendship Odin offered, and it scared me that it could be taken away.

Footfalls signaled the approach of Ma from the kitchen. "Ahh, Odin! There you are. This is our new foster kitty. Be careful with this one, okay? They told me that she can be a feisty one." Ma turned to see me crouched nearby. "Make sure you teach Freya the ropes, ok boy?" With that, she smoothed a loving hand over his head, unzipped the top of the carrier, and left.

For a moment I just sat there. The tip of Odin's silvery tail moved back and forth patiently, his gaze fixed on the carrier before him. When a head finally emerged out the top, I was dumbstruck.

Chapter 3

I couldn't believe what I was looking at. I had never seen anything like it before, and I wasn't certain I ever would again. It was a cat, at least, I thought it was. The head was followed by a body, and then a tail. The tail was the strangest thing of all.

The creature didn't have a single tuft of fur on her. The poor thing didn't even have whiskers!

In shock, I just sat as though glued to the floor. The naked cat just stood there, her beautiful olive-green eyes surveying the place. Her tail whipped agitatedly about, a tail just as naked as the rest of her, a tail that may have been a rat's tail if I didn't know better. Her skin had a mottled appearance with small patches of pink, light brown, and gray, and her nose was colored black.

Slowly, I rose from my place and approached. The cat regarded me intently, a low growl warning me to keep my distance. I took up the spot next to Odin, my side just barely touching his. "I'm confused. Why would Ma bring home a sickly cat?"

I asked. For, in my experience, only animals sick with mange and other things had no fur.

Odin kept his eyes on the newcomer as he replied. "I do not believe she is sick. I think maybe this is the way she is, just like me having one eye is the way I am."

Understanding flooded me and I relaxed a bit. I believed Odin was right. This cat was different, but it did not mean that she was sick or that we could not welcome her as best we could.

The strange cat sauntered forward, giving us wide berth as she headed for the living room. We just remained where we were, watching. It wasn't until she was almost out of sight that Odin and I moved to continue our surveillance of her. We followed into the living room and jumped up onto the back of the sofa to view her from up high. She had stopped and regarded us from unblinking peridot eyes.

She was a strange thing standing there in our living room, and it suddenly occurred to me that she probably knew that. I jumped down from my perch to the floor, then slowly moved closer... closer...

I heard no growl, but when I got too close for comfort, she hissed.

Immediately, I stopped and hunkered down, my belly against the carpet. I understood that the hiss was not an act of aggression, rather, her telling me that she felt threatened. I did not raise my hackles defensively. In fact, I struggled to remain calm and serene. I could smell her fear, and it reminded me of myself not so very long ago.

"Why are you following me?" she asked. Her voice was different, almost exotic in a pleasant sort of way. I liked it.

I cocked my head. "Well, as I see it, you are in my territory. Why would I not follow?" My words reminded me of similar ones that Odin had spoken to me when I first came to live here.

The other cat looked defensive and thoughtful at the same time. Then, "I did not choose to come here."

"Neither did I. But here I am, and here you are."

She looked at me confused, and sat back on her haunches, her skinny tail curling up over one hind leg to form a loose circle. She looked proud sitting there, regal almost, like a queen. "You did not choose to be here?"

"No, but I'm glad I am. Here I am loved. Here I am cared for."

Sadness reflected in the beautiful eyes of the other cat, as though she remembered something. Her entire demeanor shifted from a proud queen to someone who had nothing. "You are young and beautiful. No one will want an old cat like me."

I just sat there for a moment, disbelieving. Certainly, Ma would not have brought home a cat that no one would want. Certainly, there were people out there who wanted a cat like this one, even if she did have no fur. I remembered a time that I felt the same as this cat, and yet, here I was in a place where humans loved and treasured me.

Slowly, I rose from my place and approached the strange cat. She remained in her position without moving, without speaking, without making a sound of any kind. And when I was near enough, I reached out my face, closer... closer... closer... until my nose touched hers. "You are wrong. There are people who want a cat just like you. And they live right here, in this house."

Chapter 4

It wasn't until later the following day that the children came home. They seemed happy, their eyes sparkling and bright. Ma and Dad just looked tired. I watched as the two parents gave one another a look, pulled themselves together, and called out the names of their children. The dark-haired ones belonged to Ma: Arianna, Alexander, Samuel, and Ranlee. And the light-haired ones belonged to Dad: Pippin, Victoria, Todd, and Benjamin.

The children obediently returned to the foyer, everyone quiet as they trained all their attention to Ma and Dad, for it was rare that everyone was called in all at once.

"We have a visitor in the house," said Ma.

The four dark-haired children each got an excited look in their eyes as they glanced at one another. The four blond children remained quiet, looking at the other four inquiringly.

"Before your mom and I were married, she would take cats into her home and foster them until new homes could be found for them. People who foster cats and dogs like this help make more room for other animals in the shelters," said Dad.

Wide smiles of understanding took over the blond children's faces and the air of excitement now enveloped everyone.

"You should all go sit down in the living room and we will bring in the new cat. Just like when Freya first came, she will be afraid. You have to remember to speak quietly and move slowly," said Ma.

Sam scooped me up in his arms as everyone moved towards the sofas. I sat contentedly as Ma left for a moment and returned with the new cat in her arms.

Everyone's eyes got wide.

"This is called a Sphynx cat," said Ma. "Her breed is rare, so most people never see one in their entire lives except maybe in movies or in photos. She is a tortoiseshell, giving her skin a mottled look. If she had fur, it would look white, orange, and gray."

"Oh Ma!" exclaimed twelve-year-old Arianna. I want to see! Can I touch her?"

Ma smiled and walked over to Ari. "Of course, you can."

The naked cat remained still in Ma's arms, yet, I could see her trembling from where I sat ensconced in Sam's embrace beside Ari. I sent her a trill of reassurance that Sam heard. Somehow, he seemed to know what I was saying and my boy hugged me close.

Arianna's fingertips brushed across the new cat's side and the skin moved to create a series of wrinkles before smoothing out again. The girl's expression shifted from excitement to wonder. "She's so soft! She feels like warm velvet!"

Sam reached out a hand as well, and his face mimicked that of his sister. "Wow! She feels really neat!"

Then the voices of all the other children spoke up in unison.

"I want to pet her!"

"Ma! Me next!"

"What does velvet feel like again?"

When everyone had a chance to touch the newcomer, Ari asked, "What is her name?"

"I think I like Purza," said Ma. "What do you all think?"

Victoria's blue eyes sparkled. "I really like that play on the word 'purr'."

"Yeah, I like it too," said Todd.

All the other children chimed in, each one voicing their approval.

"Alright now, everyone. Time to get ready for bed," said Dad.

Groans of dismay sounded throughout the room, yet all the children did as they were bidden. That is, everyone except for Ari, who loitered at the staircase, an expression of longing on her face.

Still holding onto Purza, Ma went over to her. "What's wrong, Ari? Are you alright?"

Arianna looked at Purza, reaching out to pet the top of the naked cat's head. "She looks cold, Mama. Can she come sleep in my new room? I'll give her my warm blanket from when I was a baby."

Arianna had just recently moved out of Pippin's room downstairs to take over Victoria's room upstairs. Tori had been afraid to sleep alone, and so the girls had decided to switch places. I imagined that Ari was now having a hard time sleeping by herself. Having a cat in the room would help her.

Ma smiled affectionately. "Yes, I do believe she has been cold." She placed the trembling cat into her daughter's arms. "Go ahead and make her warm. I will bring a litter box."

Chapter 5

I lay in the center of Sam's freshly made bed, taking in the sunshine coming in through the window. Odin lay beside me, his eyes half-closed in contentment. I may have felt the same if not for the rumbling my stomach made. There had been less food in my bowl this morning. I had told Ma so, but she had simply patted my head like she always does, and continued with her chores. The hunger brought my thoughts to another time in my life, a time when I was not only hungry, but dirty and sick. There had been no soft bed to lay upon, no warm fireplace, no Odin, and no Sam.

My attention was diverted when the door to the room creaked open. Odin sat up and stretched as Purza sauntered in. She instantly found us atop the bed and effortlessly leaped up to join us. Her body language showed her disgruntlement. "Why didn't you tell me this house is *Infested*?" She emphasized the last word she spoke, making it sound ominous.

Odin and I looked at one another, then back at the naked cat. "What?" he asked.

She gave him a sidelong glare. "You know, your *problem.*" She emphasized the last word again. "I'm certain you've encountered it by now. The smell of fairies is everywhere up here."

Odin and I looked at one another once more, this time with a blossom of understanding. "Oh, you mean the goblins? They are gone now," I said. "And wasp fairies are in every house."

Purza settled down into a classic cat pose: chest out, head held high, tail curled up along her side. She looked back and forth between us as though trying to figure something out.

"You really don't know, do you."

It was more a statement than a question, yet I answered anyways. "Know what?"

"This house isn't just any house. It is located in what cats like to call a Gateway, a place where denizens from the Land of Fairies can come into the World of Humans. That makes this house, and probably many of the other houses around here, Infested."

"What exactly does that mean?" I asked.

For the first time, Purza's eyes shone with worry. She lowered her head and moved closer. Odin and I did the same, so close that our three noses almost touched. The hair on my shoulders had begun to rise, and I could feel my tail begin to bottlebrush. "It means that things from Fairy can easily come here and take up residence, things that can harm the humans who live here."

"It has always been my job to protect my humans," said Odin. "Even in the other house we lived in before this one, there were little things here and there that I kept away. It is normal."

"Not like the things I'm talking about," said Purza. "Here, there are harmful things. *Dangerous* things. The wasp fairies you mentioned are more a nuisance than anything else. The goblins can cause quite a bit of trouble, but there are things that are much, much more frightening than they."

Ma suddenly entered the room and the three of us startled apart. But that wasn't until after she'd seen us all, nose to nose. "Awww, you three are really getting along! Freya, you are doing so well accepting the new kitty. You are such a good girl!"

I accepted Ma's verbal praise, along with the loving pets she provided by giving a loud purr. Ma held my face in her hands and then kissed my nose. "I am so lucky I found you."

Ma then moved to pet Odin and Purza. She gave them both their own praises in her beautiful voice and I felt happy to be in this home. But then I felt it again, a rumbling in my stomach, and this time, it felt like it was moving. Startled, I moved to look at the offending place on my belly, laying on my side to get a good view.

The mound of my belly curved upward. I stared at it for a moment, surprised, as I licked the place where I'd felt the movement. I then regarded myself with some foreboding, because I recalled a time when I'd looked this way before.

Chapter 6

I trotted into Arianna's room, looking for Purza. I hadn't seen her all day and thought I'd look to see what the older cat might be up to. When I entered, I was greeted by the sight of a large box in the middle of the floor. To the left, Arianna sat at her desk, scribbling away on a pad of paper. Propped up before her was a big schoolbook. Just from the few moments I'd been in the room, I could sense the tension in the girl, and worry washed over me. Was she alright?

I approached the desk and sat beside Ari's chair. I looked up at the girl, taking in long dark hair and sun-bronzed skin just like Sam's. "Mrow?"

I waited for a response, but got none. I rubbed myself against Ari's leg, hoping for a pet. "Mrow?"

Still nothing.

It was so strange of Ari to not acknowledge me. I went over to the box. I would sit in it until the girl was finished with her task, then ask for more pets. I leaped inside, only to find, rather unpleasantly, that the box was already occupied.

"Rawrrr!"

Purza and I shrieked, hissed and batted at one another for a moment before we realized it was just us. The box had toppled over onto its side and Ari stopped what she was doing.

"Ugh! Freya, what are you doing in here! I don't have time for this right now. I have a project due in two days. Shoo! Get out! Shoo!"

I crouched there, aghast at Arianna's response to my being in the room. Never had she shooed me out before, never had she raised her voice to me. She saw my reaction and an expression of regret washed over her face.

"Oh, Freya! I'm sorry. Come here girl, come here." She knelt down and patted her hands on her lap. I crept over and she picked me up and cradled me in her arms the way my boy does, her face pressed alongside mine. I felt her sobbing and my heart squeezed.

What was wrong with our Arianna?

"I'm so sorry, pretty girl. Please forgive me."

I licked her face and tasted the saltiness of her tears. I wanted to tell her it was alright, and that I loved her. I gave a soft trill near Ari's ear and her crying slowly ceased. She looked at me through wet, dark brown eyes and gently smoothed the fur around my face.

"I'm just running out of time for everything and I feel sick from worrying. I'm late on all my schoolwork and this project is big. It's worth twenty percent of my grade! I can't tell Ma because I'm afraid she will be disappointed in me. I don't know what to do!"

I didn't understand everything she was saying, but I knew enough that she was in trouble. She needed to talk to Ma about her problems, but she was afraid. I wished I could speak Human so that I could tell her that Ma loved her and would want to help her. But all that came out was, "Mrow."

Ari sniffed and wiped her eyes and nose on her sleeve. She then petted me one last time before getting up, going over to her desk, and sitting back down in the chair. I looked over to Purza. The other cat was moving the box around as though trying to get it upright again. But when she couldn't, she simply walked inside.

I stepped over to the box. Crouched within the confines, Purza regarded me from half-closed eyes. "I'm sorry. I didn't know you were in here before."

"I know that, Freya. You just startled me is all. Come, sit with me."

Purza made room for me, and once I was situated, we rested together. With her side pressed against mine, I could feel each breath she took. Without fur there, I could feel the breaths better than I could when it was Odin. I wondered if she liked the feel of my fur, and if it gave her the warmth she craved.

For a while we just sat there. I felt myself starting to feel good, just like I always did when I'd been sitting in a box, and I felt energetic. Purza seemed to feel the same. I could tell by the fine stretching she did when she rose from her place beside me, the shine in her eyes, and the spring to her step when she exited the box.

I rose from my place as well. "You seem almost ..." I struggled for the word, "... rejuvenated."

Purza gave me an intense look, almost as though she was trying to figure out exactly what I was getting at. "Of course. No different than you."

I became thoughtful. "I suppose I feel the same way. I've just never considered it before."

Purza cocked her head. "Why not? It's an important thing for any cat to consider."

I looked at the older cat, suddenly feeling like I was missing something. She noticed my perplexity and rubbed her face against mine in a gesture of affection. "Come, bedtime is near, and you need to get to your boy."

In acquiescence, I began to follow her out, but then saw Purza looking at the girl sitting sadly in her chair. I saw the caring reflected in the cat's eyes and my heart melted a little bit at the sight.

Arianna had become Purza's girl just like Sam was my boy.

Chapter 7

The three of us sat before the fireplace, the flames within casting shifting shadows on the walls throughout the darkened room. The living room had a feeling to it I couldn't describe, a feel that made me keep looking into the spaces where the firelight couldn't reach.

"This house has such darkness to it," whispered Purza, her skin wrinkling up as though she'd felt something touch her.

"I have sensed that on occasion, but I believe the love of this family keeps some of it at bay," replied Odin.

Purza regarded us with utmost solemnity. "I have already started taking measures against one of the dangers." She turned to give me all of her attention. "It's why I was in the box."

I gave her a piercing look. "What does that have to do with anything?" I looked at Odin and then back at Purza. "I don't understand."

Purza looked at me speculatively for a moment. "How long were you with your mother?"

Amber eyes floated into my range of vision, beautiful eyes filled with love and devotion. The feel of her raspy tongue, the softness of her white fur, the warmth of the milk she offered. Her voice was like none other I'd ever heard since, and her scent was what I imagined heaven might smell like.

I didn't understand the relevancy of the question, yet I sadly answered it. "Not for very long. She'd said there was so much she wanted to teach my brothers and I, but she never had the chance. One day we were just taken away and we never saw her again."

I looked at my companions and both had expressions of sadness and understanding. Purza reached out a paw and touched me gently on my face. "You were taken from her too young. You never had the chance to learn many important things, but I will teach you."

"I will help," said Odin. "If I had known..."

"Teach me what?" I interrupted.

"About how to fight the things in the darkness," said Odin. "You did so well against the goblins, I thought you knew. It seems to come very naturally to you." He purred and rubbed his head against my side. "Like I said, you are special."

I preened at his praise, but my eyes remained on the older cat. The way the firelight played about on her furless body was almost breathtaking. If I didn't know her better, I'd have thought her to be one of those things from The Land of Fairies, a creature of mystery and shadows. But, looking at her eyes, I could see her light and her dedication to help us and the humans who lived in this house.

"So, what is it about the box?" I asked. "You make it sound like it is important."

Purza's peridot eyes widened and her voice became enthusiastic. "Oh, it IS important. You see, it is the boxes that give many of these dangerous things we've spoken about their power."

I felt my own eyes widen as well.

"You've noticed how good you feel after sitting in a box. You used the perfect word for it just this evening. *Rejuvenated.* It is because you have taken the power of that box unto yourself."

"Just by sitting in it?" I asked, astounded.

"Yes, just by sitting in it."

Purza's tone became grim. "However, the creatures from Fairy can also sit in the box. They can also take the power. It is in this way that the creatures can stay in the World of Humans longer. It is in this way that they can cause more harm."

"So, we have to sit in the box first," I said.

"Exactly," affirmed Purza.

"Well, with Christmas so near, there will be boxes everywhere," said Odin.

Purza gave a swish of her tail. "And that will mean more trouble."

"Christmas?" I'd heard the word maybe once or twice, but didn't know what it meant.

"It is a day when humans give each other boxes and bags filled with things that make them happy," said Odin. "It is a day of great joy."

A sat there for a moment, wondering. What day could possibly be better than a day spent with Odin and being loved by my boy?

Chapter 8

"Everyone! Time for dinner! called Ma.

From all around the house they came, the quick pattering of feet against the floor as the children gathered into the dining room around a table large enough for all ten family members. As everyone patiently waited, Ma continued to put the remaining dishes of food on the table with the help of the eldest girl, Pippin, and Sam had just finished setting the plates.

Finally, everyone was seated, everyone except one person.

"Where is Ari?" asked Dad.

It was silent for a moment before Alex spoke up. "I think she might be in her room doing her homework."

Ma nodded. "She probably didn't hear me. Please go and get her."

Alex rose and left the table only to come back a couple of minutes later. "She says she's not hungry."

Ma looked at Dad, her brows pulled together in concern. I could tell she was tempted to get up and talk to Ari, but she remained seated and began to eat with the rest of the family.

Interest piqued, I rose from my spot on the back of one of the sofas and leapt down. Upon landing I felt myself get a little off balance, but I recovered swiftly and trotted up the stairs to Arianna's room. Once there, I pushed open the door and was met with the sight of the girl sitting in the middle of the floor. Spread before her was a large square of poster board upon which had been drawn various images, and off to the side was an array of brightly colored markers. Purza intently watched the goings-on with avid interest, her black-tipped ears pointed forward.

I walked over to Purza and lay down beside her. Together we just watched for a while, but it didn't take long before my eyes began to close as lethargy overtook me.

"Purza, no. You can't sit on my project, girl." I opened my eyes to see Arianna scooping up the naked cat and setting her to the side. "Now you stay there."

Purza proceeded to do as she was bidden and sat back on her haunches. Her eyes were wide and her ears swiveled here and there as though she was trying to hear something. Meanwhile, Arianna worked apace, and I could feel the tension in her body as she endeavored to complete the work before her.

I heard familiar footsteps and so I was expecting Ma when she entered the room. "Oh Ari, your project is beautiful!"

The girl gave a tired smile. "Thanks Ma."

"You almost finished?"

Arianna hesitated before answering, and I felt a spike in her tension. "Almost."

"Well, you need to come down and eat, okay? I left a plate for you on the island."

The girl had returned her eyes to the poster board and was getting back to work. "Alright."

Satisfied with that response, Ma then left the room. Once the sound of her footsteps had faded, Arianna looked up from her project and at the door her mother had just passed through. Sadness shone in her eyes and then her face distorted into a small grimace as she clutched a hand to her belly.

She looked back down at the poster, a tear dripping down onto one of the images. Her whisper was so soft, even my feline ears struggled to pick up the words. "I'll never have enough time to get this done."

Chapter 9

The next morning the house was abuzz as the children got ready for school. The other two older kids, Pippin and Victoria, had already eaten breakfast and had left to catch the bus when Arianna hurried down the stairs. She wore the same jeans and shirt as the day before, her hair was pulled into a haphazard ponytail, and there were dark circles beneath her eyes.

Ma walked in just as Arianna pulled her backpack over her shoulders and was about to rush out the door. "Hey there Ari! Why didn't you eat your dinner last night? It was still on the island this morning when I came down."

Arianna gave a weak smile. "Sorry, I just wasn't hungry. Gotta go!" And with that, she was out the door and running after the older girls.

Ma just stood there for a moment, her brows knit. She then shook her head and closed the door. Feeling Ma's worry, I twined myself about her legs in a show of affection. "Mrow."

With a sad smile, Ma stooped to pet me along the top of my head and back before tending to the younger children that were still getting ready for school

"Something was there," said Purza.

I turned to look at the other cat in puzzlement. "What was where?"

"Something was in Ari's room last night."

"What was it?"

"I'm not sure. But whatever it was, I could feel it trying to do something when it got close to Arianna."

Odin walked up to join us, touching his nose to mine and Purza's in greeting. "When I did my rounds last night, I saw that the light was still on in Arianna's room. It was very late."

Purza gave a slow swish of her tail that demonstrated her agreement. "I want to show you both something."

Odin and I followed the other cat to Ari's room. The curtains were drawn, so our eyes had to acclimate to the darkness, and the ominous feeling of something amiss washed over us. Purza led us over to one corner of the girl's dresser. The space around it was cluttered, as though someone had tossed a bunch of things there on purpose. Purza dug through those things until she reached what she was looking for. She grabbed onto it with her teeth and pulled. And pulled. And pulled. Odin and I watched until a poster board came into view.

Purza stepped away and joined us to look at Arianna's project. Beautiful images graced the poster, images that looked so real I was tempted to reach out and touch them. There were butterflies and caterpillars, fishes and small round globes, frogs and smaller versions of them with tails. There was an image of a cat with her kittens, and an outline of what appeared to be a human mother with her baby. There were words next to the pictures, and those ended halfway down the poster.

It was obvious that Ari's project was unfinished.

"My girl cried as she hid the poster here." Purza's voice was mournful. "She then proceeded to sit at her desk and look at all of her books until sleep claimed her. "

I looked over at my new friend. Purza's head drooped, and her eyes were lackluster. "You stayed awake with her, didn't you," I stated.

"I did my best. But something was here with us into the night, something bad." Purza shook at the memory. And it was fast... so fast I couldn't get a good look at it."

"What did Ari do when it was close to her?" asked Odin.

Purza was thoughtful. "She looked like she might have been reading what was on the page of her book. But, now that I think about it, she was just staring ahead. When I jumped up on the desk, she would blink her eyes, look at her clock, and mumble about it getting too late and that she was running out of time."

I just sat there for a moment, thoughts racing through my mind. I spoke my final thought aloud.

"It's almost like, whatever this thing is, it's stealing time from Arianna."

Odin looked back and forth between me and Purza. "It sounds like we might need to try and catch ourselves a time thief."

Chapter 10

Arianna stood at the entry to the bedroom that Todd and Alex shared. "Will you do my chores today?"

Alexander looked up at his sister past the top edge of his small laptop, his expression deadpan, his lips pulled into a thin line. "Why do you always ask me? What about everyone else?"

Arianna frowned. "Everyone else is busy with homework or soccer."

Alex frowned. "And I'm not busy?"

"Pleeeeease," she begged. "I'll pay you back."

Alex's frown deepened. "I've done your chores for the past week."

"I've just had too much schoolwork. And tonight, I'm supposed to vacuum. You know how long that takes."

"Yeah, I know." He gave a gusty sigh. "I can't do it, Ari. Not this time. I have a test tomorrow." He looked back down at his laptop.

"C'mon Alex. You're the only one I've got." Her voice was pleading.

Alex remained silent behind his computer screen.

With tears in her eyes, Ari left. I followed as she went down the hall to get the vacuum cleaner out of the closet. She unloosed the cord and started the machine. The loud *whirr* startled me into a scamper up onto the sofa. From there I watched, and it wasn't long before I noticed something.

At first, I thought it was a shadow. It blended so well within the dimness offered by the folds of the curtains. But then it shifted slightly, giving me a glimpse of its shape.

It was then I saw it better. Just knowing the shape of the thing made it so much clearer.

It was a little man. He had no color, only shades of gray. His most distinguishing feature was his long beard, closely followed by the crumpled cap he wore. It looked like it had once stood straight and tall, like a cone. From this distance, he looked like he stood as high as me, and that he was slightly rounded about his middle.

Running the vacuum along the carpet, Arianna moved closer and closer to the curtain where the little man stood. Meanwhile, I slowly got myself into position from my perch on the couch, waiting... waiting... waiting. Ari got closer, and still I continued to wait. Finally, she was beside the window. The curtain shifted and I saw the creature hold up his hands. What looked like a little strike of lightening flashed...

...and the world stopped.

Well, not really. It didn't really stop. But it kind of looked like it.

In awe, I remained where I was as the world around me shifted and wavered, almost like it was underwater. I saw Alex come down the stairs and go into the kitchen, moving the same way he always does. Meanwhile, Arianna looked like she was moving in slow motion, so slow it was like trying to walk in a deep pool of thick mud. Todd and Ben passed by, shaking their heads because the sound of the vacuum was too loud for them to play their game. Alex went back up the stairs. Ma went past with a basketful of laundry.

And suddenly it was over. The bubble popped and Arianna put the vacuum away. She looked at the clock over the mantle and squeezed her hands into fists before darting upstairs to her room.

I didn't move from my place on the sofa. I narrowed my eyes and watched the little man move from shadow to shadow, slowly moving in the same direction the girl had taken.

Chapter 11

Odin stared at me, his eye unblinking. "You let it get away?"

I sat back on my haunches, offended. This reminded me of another scenario not so long ago when Odin had said the same thing about the goblins. "Of course, it got away! I was trapped in the same quagmire as Ari."

But the thing was, I hadn't even tried to get the little man hiding in the curtain. For all I knew, I could have sprinted across the room, grabbed him in my jaws, and torn him to pieces. Instead, I'd just sat there, captivated by the magic all around me, studying what was happening.

And it was then I remembered being able to turn my head and I recalled the swishing of my tail against the sofa cushion. Was I immune from effects of the magic because I had seen the little man?

"It sounds like a gnome," said Purza. "But different."

"What is a gnome?" asked Odin. "And different how?"

"Well, all of the gnomes I have seen and heard about are harmless creatures from the Land of the Fairies. Their clothing is brightly colored, they like to wear tall, conical hats, and the men have thick beards. They sometimes come to the World of Humans, but only to steal little things that have been left laying around for a while, things that will probably never be missed. Some will even take underwear and socks that have been left under the bed for too long."

I sniffed at the humor in the statement. "Underwear?"

"Oh yes. I've heard tell they are used as flags."

I regarded Purza intently at the absurdity of that statement, but she continued as though it was commonplace. "However, the gnome you speak about is cloaked in shadow and gloom."

"He isn't just taking little things around the house," said Odin. "He is taking away time, causing substantial harm to Arianna."

"But why her? Why isn't he taking time from anyone else?" I asked.

The other two cats were quiet, thoughtful.

I had an idea. "I think we should go to see the princess of the fairies. She helped us last time with Sam's nightmares. Maybe she can help us with Arianna's stolen time as well."

"As much as I would like to see the Land of the Fairies," said Purza, "you will need to go without me. I need to remain here and help my girl all I can."

The three of us swiftly ascended the stairs, and once at the top, we parted ways: Purza to Ari's room and Odin and I to Sam's. Once there, I stood before the desk upon which there was a tall bookcase. It dominated the farthest wall of the bedroom. I hadn't climbed it in a while and a feeling of uncertainty washed over me.

"Here Freya!" Sam made a soft ticking sound in his mouth and patted the blankets. I turned away from the bookcase and jumped onto his bed. He was ready for rest, clothed in his warmest pajamas and covered with his warmest blankets.

I settled down against Sam's side and the boy pulled the covers up to his chin as Ma came into the room. She bent down to give him a kiss on his forehead. "Good night, Sammy." She paused to smooth her hand over my fur. "Good night, Freya. I love you both."

With that, Ma turned out the lights and closed the door until there was barely a crack. A nightlight near the foot of Sam's bed gave off a soft luminescent glow in the shape of a star. The lights in the hallway went out soon after, and it wasn't long before Sam's breathing became slow and even as he fell into slumber.

I rose from my place and jumped down from the bed. Odin was already standing before the desk. He vaulted atop it, then proceeded to climb up the bookcase. He made it up to the top without knocking anything over. He looked down at me, head cocked, before I realized he was waiting for me to join him.

I leaped onto the desk easily enough. Yet, I felt that I was off-balance somehow, not quite as agile as I was when I first climbed the bookcase. Looking at it now, I felt the same feelings of doubt I'd had earlier.

"You coming, darling?"

A sensation of warmth came over me when I heard the term of endearment. It made me feel special. Loved. Gauging the distance and attempting to take into account the changes in my body, I leaped onto the first shelf, swiftly followed by the second. When I got onto the third, I heard something fall onto the desk and then to the carpeted floor below. I was relieved when I leaped to the top and stood beside Odin, looking down to see that Sam remained undisturbed.

Together, we stepped to the far end of the bookcase. High above, the ceiling met the wall, and where the walls met, there was a corner. A strange scent clung there, drifting down to give us a whiff here and there as we looked up. And then, just by thinking of the hole, it was there, a circular opening forming in the ceiling. It was the size of a softball, the edges jagged and undefined, shifting and wavering in the glow given off by Sam's nightlight.

Odin crouched and sprang upward. Just like the last time we entered the hole, his front paws caught onto the edge and he hung there, suspended, the curve of his lithe form casting a shadow onto the adjacent wall. And then his back legs were pedaling, seeking traction on the wall in front of him while he crawled forward with the front two.

Finally, one back paw reached the mouth of the hole, followed by the other. The hole distorted, changing shape as it stretched to fit around Odin's body before he was out of sight. I sat there for a moment, waiting. And when his head poked through the hole, he said, “Okay, it's your turn now."

I crouched low, ready to spring, but then I hesitated. Once again, the doubt was there, eating at my mind. I hissed, shoving it away, and I jumped upward with all my strength.

The instant my back paws left the surface of the bookshelf, I knew I was in trouble. My balance was all wrong, and I felt heavier than I did the last time I'd jumped so high. One of my front paws barely skimmed the edge of the hole before I was falling, falling, falling...

I twisted in midair, trying to right myself. I gave a strangled cry when I hit the floor, my head and shoulders taking the brunt of the impact. I heard Odin's response from above, and a split second later he was next to me, his voice fraught with worry. "Freya? Freya, are you alright?"

Sam was out of bed and at my side an instant later. "Girl? Oh, my poor girl! Did you fall?" His gentle hands ran over me and I mewled piteously when he picked me up, and I curved my tail between my legs. "Here, you come to bed with me now. I'll hold you."

Sam carefully put me on the bed, and after he'd made a nest with his blankets, he lay me in it. He then curved his body around me. "I'll keep you safe here with me, girl."

Odin curled up on my other side and we all rested there. My body ached, and my head felt muzzy after the fall, but I went to sleep feeling safe and loved.

Chapter 12

Odin hovered around me, the abrupt movements of his tail expressing his anxiety and concern. "I don't want to leave you. My place is here at your side."

I looked up at Odin from the nest Sam had prepared for me last night after my fall. I was still a bit sore and tired, and there was no way I could reach the hole. That meant he needed to go without me.

I purred and rubbed my face along his. "I will be fine napping here until your return." I looked at Purza curled up at my back. "Arianna is at school. Maybe you can accompany Odin to the Land of the Fairies. I am nervous for him to go alone."

Purza rose from her place and touched her nose to mine. "Yes, I will go. You will be safe here and Odin will be safe with a friend at his side."

Odin regarded me intently as he sniffed around my face and along by body. He paused at my backside near the base of my tail, his mouth open to capture the full range of his olfactory sense. His tail swished with increased agitation.

"Arianna needs us to help her. This is the only way," I said.

"Fine, I will go. But only because you ask it of me. Stay here and don't move from this place. When I return, you must promise to eat the food Ma set out for you."

"I will be here."

I watched as the two cats climbed the bookcase. Purza was the epitome of agility, scaling the tall furniture without a pause. And when they were in the correct position, and the hole appeared, my friends leaped into it.

For a while I just lay there. I looked around the room, taking in the familiarity of it. In particular, I took note of the feathered dream catcher that hung on the wall behind Sam's bed. Its magic was still strong, keeping away the goblins that used to take away all of his good dreams.

The Time Swiper

I lay my head down on the blankets. Truth was, I didn't feel well. I hadn't bothered to eat breakfast that morning. My belly ached, and I continuously licked the base of my tail clean of the blood-tinged fluid that seeped from there.

I rested and time began to have less meaning. A feeling of intense fatigue swept over me and I dreamed. The little gray man was there. At first, I saw him across the room, perched on the edge of the desk, his legs dangling down. The next time I opened my eyes he was closer, crouched on the top of the chair, his stance almost predatory. The next time he was closer still, peeking over the side of the bed, his crumpled hat slumped to the side of his head. The last time I opened my eyes he was right next to me. The hairs of his beard were blackened at the ends and his eyes were black as pitch. Soulless. A feeling of danger overwhelmed me. His lips moved as though he was saying something, and then there was a flash that looked like lightening.

I felt the beating inside of me slow down and it was suddenly difficult to breathe. I tried to move but it was too much. All I managed was one paw, and I reached closer, closer, closer...

And then the images of the room around me faded and there was just darkness.

Chapter 13

"Freya."

A beautiful singsong voice called out to me and I swiveled my ears towards the sound.

"Freya, I can help you, but you must come to me."

I was very tired, and all I wanted was to sleep in peace. But something about the voice was familiar, and it persistently urged me to open my eyes. A part of me wanted to. I wanted to see who the beautiful voice belonged to. It was so familiar!

"Freya, come to me, girl. I know you are tired, but come and I will give you the strength to go on."

I resisted. It was warm where I was, curled up in this place. I wanted rest.

"Freya, Sam is waiting here for you. You can see him again, but you must come now."

At the mention of my boy's name, I opened my eyes. All around there was darkness. It weighed on me, pressing me down like a blanket that was much too heavy. It was slowly suffocating me. A part of me wanted to struggle free of it, but I was so very tired.

"Freya, you must come now. It is your last chance. You must fight, or you will never see Sam again."

And then I felt something deep inside of me. I wanted to see my boy. I wanted to feel his arms around me and hear his voice in my ear. The want became a need, and the need became a passion as I struggled against the oppressiveness surrounding me. I took a breath and by body ached, but I fought through it and took another breath. I felt the beating inside me again, and it was then I realized it was the beating of my life...

I opened my eyes. Standing around me were my friends, Odin and Purza. Beside them was a girl of about twelve years- Maeve, the princess of the fairies. I looked at her in wonder. "It was your voice I heard calling to me."

She smiled and I was enveloped by the glow of her beauty. Curly red hair tumbled past narrow shoulders down to a slim waist clothed in a shimmering pale green dress. Vivid blue eyes regarded me with the utmost of affection, and the semi-transparent wings sprouting from her upper back fluttered fiercely to produce a dust that surrounded us in a glittery haze.

Maeve reached out and placed her hand onto my swollen belly. Her beautiful smile widened as she felt what lay within, and I realized that she knew my secret. "Odin and Purza came to me. They spoke of a gray gnome and I asked where you were. When they told me that you were unable to accompany them, and that you had been left here, I came as swiftly as possible."

I turned to look at my friends. Odin regarded me with the utmost devotion, and Purza's tender gaze told me the depth of her love as well. The older cat put a paw against my face. "We thought you had gone and left us."

"I will be eternally grateful to Maeve," said Odin as he looked at the fairy princess. "She knew the danger you were in and it was her magic that brought you back to us."

"All I remember is getting more and more tired," I said. "The gray man was there, getting closer and closer. I sensed that he was a thing borne of wickedness."

"He is a Time Swiper," said Maeve, "a gnome that has been corrupted by evil. He takes time from others and brings it unto himself. It brings him the immortality he desires." The fairy swept her hand over my belly back towards my tail. It hovered at the base before lifting, and her wings ceased their fluttering. All around, the glittery dust just hovered.

"Time Swipers like to prey upon a single person," continued Maeve. "The more worn down the person becomes, the more easily the Swiper can steal their time."

"How does one overcome such an adversary?" asked Odin.

"Time Swipers are beings of great darkness. The only way to defeat one is with the power of light." Maeve's voice became grim. "You must be very careful. They gain the most power when they steal time from something that is sick or injured." She looked down at me. "They will prey upon that person or animal until there is hardly any time left to give. And in the end, if death occurs, the Swiper gains power tenfold."

Silence filled the bedroom as all present looked at me. I looked from one solemn face to the next, taking in the ramifications of Maeve's words. "So, if left unchecked, the gray man can cause Arianna's death."

The twinkling dust had begun to subside, the healing atmosphere having done its work. "Yes," replied the princess. "Just like he almost caused yours."

Chapter 14

From my place on the sofa I preferred most, I watched the children. They seemed happier than usual, their voices raised in excitement as they played together in the living room. There was a board situated in the middle of the floor. It was marked with brightly colored images and a series of squares that formed a path. It was upon that path the children had placed little pieces that they moved around. Everyone was there, even Ranlee who was too young to play.

Everyone except Arianna.

The girl sat alone on the sofa nearest the fireplace. She had her legs pulled up beneath her, and her arms crossed before her chest as though she was cold. Covering her feet was a blanket, and laying upon it was Purza. The naked cat looked lonely sitting there, but I knew if I moved over there to keep her company, it was less likely that Arianna would pick Purza up to sit on her lap.

So, I stayed where I was and I watched. I remembered what had happened earlier that day when Arianna had come home from school. The girl had missing homework, and it had caused her grades to be low. Ma and Dad were upset. They might have punished her, but they could see how upset Arianna was already. Nothing had happened after that, but Ari kept apart. Alex and Sam looked over at her a time or two, but not knowing what to do, they turned back to the game in front of them.

Odin walked by the sofa and I watched as he passed. Tension exuded from him, and his tail was held high in alert. His ears swiveled to catch every possible sound in the room, and his single golden eye kept track of every movement. I could tell that he was still rattled by what had happened earlier in the day. He kept looking at me as though to be certain I was really there. Purza explained how their arrival had frightened the gray gnome away, and that I had looked so unnatural all stretched out, as though I'd been reaching for something...

Without a sound, Arianna abruptly rose from the sofa and vacated the room. Purza and I shared a look before she hopped down from her spot to follow. I rose to do the same when Odin was suddenly there before me, his tail swishing back and forth, his gaze intense.

Startled, I fell back onto my haunches. The hairs on my neck rose as I met his eye. He looked intimidating standing there before me, and I wondered what I'd done to earn his ire.

"You will stay here," he said.

"But Purza needs my help," I objected.

Odin growled, a sound he'd never directed at me before. "You will stay here where it is safer."

I shrank away from him, hating the feelings he provoked, most notably fear. Yet, I would not back down and my hackles rose. My tone was obstinate. "I will go where I please."

He growled again. "You will not leave this spot."

I was a flurry of motion. I growled and spat, lifting my paw to swat him neatly across the face: once, twice, three times. And then I was rushing from the sofa. I was almost to the staircase, when Odin streaked past to block my way.

We stood there, backs arched, tails puffed. We both growled and I spat again. I was about to reach out to strike Odin once more when I felt a familiar pair of hands under my front legs lifting me up.

"Hey pretty girl. What's going on, hunh?" My boy cradled me in his arms and I instantly began to calm. Sam brought me into the kitchen and he sat down with me in the quiet that pervaded the dimly lit room. He petted me and spoke in his most soothing voice, running his hands over the top of my head, my face, and my neck.

Finally, I relaxed. Sam continued to pet me for a moment before putting me down on the closest chair. He said, "I love you, girl," before striding away back into the living room.

I stretched before laying down on the chair. Strangely, Odin was nowhere to be seen. My thoughts went to Purza alone upstairs with Arianna. The need to be with my friend washed over me, but I was tired. Maybe I would rest here for just a moment...

I must have dozed, because the next thing I knew, my eyes were snapping open and I was in a state of increased awareness. The kitchen was dark, but I could still hear the activity of my family in the living room. I looked around, and despite the lack of light, I could see him.

The gray gnome.

He slowly moved along the wall towards the basement door. It wasn't entirely closed, open just a crack. Most of the time, Ma would close it when she was finished with the laundry for the day. But today... today it had somehow been left open. The little man moved <u>purposefully</u> towards it, and once at the door, he slipped within the crack and down into the basement.

For a moment I just sat there. I hated the basement. It had a bad feeling about it, not to mention that it was <u>musty</u> and damp. It was so dark, that even my superior feline sight found it hard to see. It was a place that I didn't want to revisit, but the gray gnome had gone down there.

Without another thought, I leaped down from the chair. I slowly approached the basement, looking toward the living room where my humans laughed and played. I could pick out my boy's voice. I took that voice and held it close, wrapped it around me like the blanket that he shared with me every night.

And then I slipped through the door.

Chapter 15

A familiar musty smell surrounded me as I padded down the wooden stairs. The air became noticeably cooler, and my paws felt the chill of the place the moment they stepped onto the hard ground at the bottom. I moved deeper into the darkness, following the scent I had come to expect in the presence of the gray gnome. I passed stacks of dilapidated boxes, aged furniture, and a jumble of other things strewn here and there. Faint traces of light filtered in through small glass block windows near the ceiling that were obscured by old, torn spider webs thick with accumulated dust.

It all looked familiar, for I had been in this place before. I had felt the *wrongness* of it.

I turned a corner and found myself in another room of the basement. It was also filled with decrepit things long forgotten. Ma and Dad never came here; even the floor looked like it hadn't been trod upon in many years. Here, the feeling of wrongness was heavier. Here, the scent of bad fairy things was stronger.

Bad fairy things. Yes, that was accurate. Bad things from the Land of the Fairies came here. I wasn't sure I wanted to know what they were doing in this place.

My hackles rose. I sniffed at the stale air and continued onward. A myriad of smells tackled my olfactory sense. It reminded me of the goblins I'd experienced before, the gray gnome that was causing so much trouble now, and many others that I simply didn't know. I followed the scents and they got stronger and stronger. I followed them to the far wall and then stopped. Slowly, I turned to look to my left.

It was still there- the broken bookshelf. The thing had toppled over and the top edge of it leaned against the wall. The overwhelming sense of wrongness made my skin crawl, yet I padded closer to it. It was dark in that space the shelf made where it leaned against the wall, darker than anywhere else in the basement. A part of me didn't want to go in, sensing danger there. Yet, the other part of me was compelled. I had come here for a reason, and she sat upstairs in her bedroom right now, sad and forlorn.

Slowly, I approached the dark opening. I remembered the last time I'd been there, remembered what lay within, remembered the creepy feeling that had come over me. I had turned on my hind feet and run back through the basement, up the stairs and to the door where I'd huddled the rest of the night. I paused before the opening, every sense on highest alert, and then I walked in.

Within this darkest of places, my vision struggled. I continued further... further... further. And then I stopped and looked all around. Where I had once remembered a pile of human teeth that stood almost as high as I did tall, there was nothing. Flabbergasted, I just stood there. Had I imagined it? Had my imagination truly concocted something so macabre?

I put my nose to the ground and started sniffing. I looked closely as I moved along, searching for anything that might show me that, indeed, an eerie mound of human teeth had once been there.

Finally, I found it. One lonely tooth lay near some rubble created when the shelf collapsed. I stared at it almost gleefully, glad I wasn't going crazy after all. I was about to pick it up with my teeth when I heard him.

"Freya? Darling, are you down here?"

I stopped, my ears pricking towards the distant sound of Odin's voice.

"Freya, I'm sorry we fought. If you are down here, please come out. I am worried about you." His voice was tinged with a hint of desperation.

I felt torn. I really wanted to continue to investigate this space beneath the fallen bookcase. But Odin was looking for me, and he was making so much noise. The elusive gray gnome was certainly gone by now.

I left the tooth and went back the way I had come, navigating around the piles of junk and other things that made up this awful place. All the while,

I couldn't help feeling that something, or someone, was watching me, and every once in a while, I'd turn to look and find nothing there.

"Freya, if you are here, please answer. You must believe me when I say I'm sorry. I lo..."

I paused when Odin's voice abruptly stopped. A sense of foreboding swept over me and I peered into a part of the basement I'd never been before, where I'd last heard Odin's voice coming from. The fur rose all along my spine, and this time, I *knew* I was being watched. I abruptly turned, and there, staring at me from the dark, was the Time Swiper.

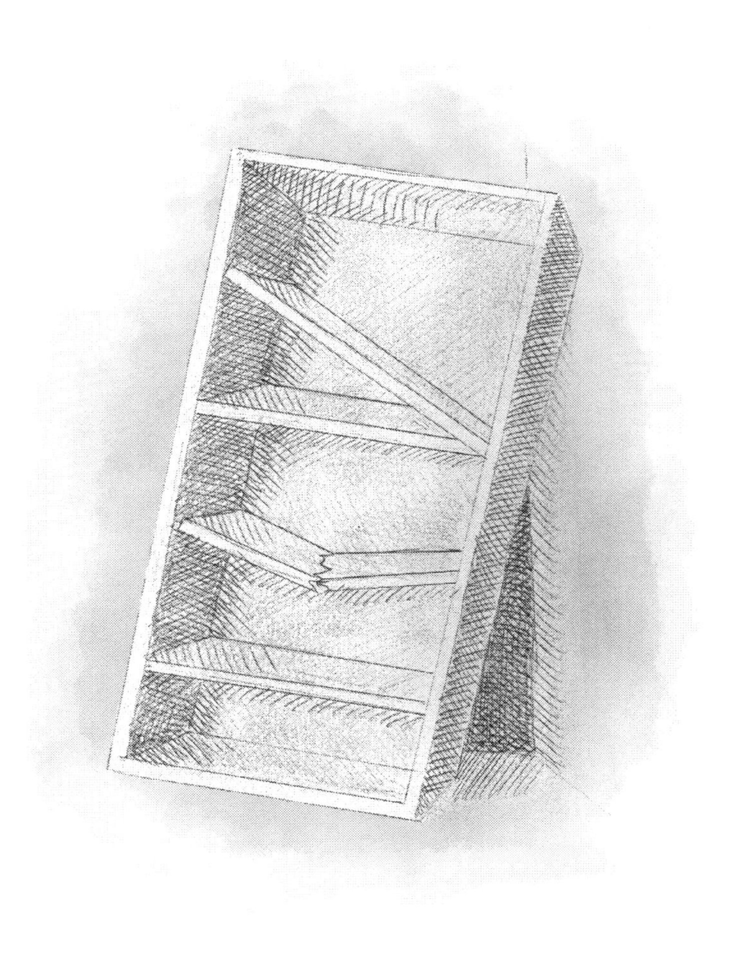

Chapter 16

I went still, the hairs all over my body rising to stand on end. I could feel the vile malevolence of the creature before me, imagined the atrocities he had visited upon others. There wasn't a doubt in my mind that he had killed before; that was why it was so easy for him to make me his target.

Slowly, I started to back away. He wore a dark gray shirt and lighter gray pants. Dangling from the black belt around his rotund waist were three gray pouches. They looked full and I couldn't help wondering what they contained. He watched me with a sinister intensity, and after a few moments he stepped forward.

Back and back I went into the unexplored part of the basement, the gray gnome following. I dared not turn away, and I'm not certain I could have. I was captivated by those dark soulless eyes. I watched his every move. Somehow, he looked different than he had in Sam's bedroom yesterday. He looked darker, more shadowed.

I don't know how far we moved, but it was far enough when I felt the wall of something pressing against my backside. A quick glance showed towering things on both sides of me. Fear took hold as I realized I had been backed into a corner and there was nowhere for me to go. I was trapped.

Then from out of nowhere, there was a streak of shadow. It hurtled towards the gray gnome and struck him in the side. I heard a deep feline growl as the gnome went down, and I knew who had come to my aid.

It was Odin.

"Rawwr!" I surged forward and didn't hesitate to enter the fray, instantly feeling the strength of our opponent as he struck me away with little more than a sweep of his arm. I heard Odin shriek in rage as I went sprawling across the floor, my fur picking all manner of dust and debris before I slid to a stop. I leaped to my feet and rushed back to find that Odin had latched onto the gnome. The creature screamed, yanking at Odin to try and dislodge him. Fear for my friend gave me wings. I leaped onto the enemy and landed onto his back.

The crumpled cone hat the gnome wore toppled from his head...

...and that was when things started to go horribly wrong.

I heard a sound like the scattering of a hundred small rocks and the gnome roared. Strong hands ripped me from his back and I found myself soaring through the air. My landing was broken by a pile of boxes. They toppled over when I struck, and for a moment I struggled to get myself free of them and back on my feet. The scene that met my eyes was like something I might see on the box with the moving pictures the children liked to look at.

The gnome wasn't just a gnome anymore. He was a shadow monster. He stood at least twice as tall, with his long beard down to his feet, and clawed elongated fingers. Bright pricks of light glowed from his dark eyes, and when he opened his mouth into a rictus, rows of sharp black teeth were exposed. Laying all around his feet were the missing polished white teeth.

I could sense the danger we faced. It was so palpable, it was like a creature of its own. Odin rose from where he'd fallen and raced towards me. "Freya, run! Run!"

But it was too late.

The gnome was fast, faster than anything I'd ever seen before. He was a blur as he began to run around us in circles, faster... faster... faster. Odin and I collapsed against one another as the gnome continued. For how long, I cannot say, but the moment he stopped, we found our chance.

Odin and I ran like our tails were afire. We ran to the staircase, streaked up the steps, and flew through the door that Ma had mercifully left open.

Chapter 17

Odin and I huddled together under the safety of the sofa, trembling. Our family sat around that sofa: Ma, Dad, all eight children, and Purza.

"They were down in the basement all this time," said Ma. "I can't believe it. They hate it down there!"

"All that searching I did outside," said Dad. "All that going from house to house asking if anyone had seen them."

"All that crying we all did," moaned Victoria.

"Ben and I turned our bedroom inside out looking for them," mentioned Todd.

"Sammy didn't eat all day," said Ranlee.

"Purza didn't either," replied Arianna.

As we sat there, listening to our family, we began to realize something. Odin and I hadn't been gone for just an hour or two. We had been gone an entire day. The Time Swiper had stolen it.

Finally, we emerged from our hiding place and into the waiting arms of those who loved us most. My boy sobbed and held me tight as though he never wanted to let me go. Ma held Odin close and her eyes were bright with unshed tears. Arianna and the other children petted us and showered us with words of endearment. They then all sat down on the sofas and turned on the picture box to watch something with lots of music that made them smile and laugh. Odin, Purza and I sat among them, luxuriating in the love we felt all around us. And we slept.

The next morning the family was up bright and early. Ma started her cooking right away and before long, savory aromas wafted throughout the house. Music played over the living room speakers, and the tree was brightly lit with a multitude of gaily wrapped gifts beneath it. The children were merry and dressed in festively colored garments. Everyone went out of their way to be kind to one another. "It is a day of celebration," Odin said, "a day when people spend time with family and friends... the ones who mean the most in their lives." It was Christmas Eve.

I felt restless. I spent much of my day wandering around the house, searching... searching for the best place. I went into all of the bedrooms, all of the closets, all of bathrooms. I leaped on top of all of the beds and burrowed into all of the piles of clothes I could find laying about in the children's rooms. I even investigated the pile of soft plushy toys in Ranlee's room. Odin followed aimlessly behind, bewildered by my behavior. I said nothing and just allowed him to trail along.

The feeling was familiar. I had felt it once before in another life.

I remembered it like it was yesterday. The blond-haired boy who had loved me so dearly was gone. I remembered the fighting of the humans, the packing away of the house, and then being put out with the trash that was left over. I was hungry and alone. The toms gave me trouble. After, I wandered the streets. I got sick. Some kind people found me and took me to the place where Ma and Dad ultimately picked me up. The kittens I had birthed were still and lifeless...

In spite of my indecisiveness, I wandered back into the living room. It was nice and toasty with a fire blazing in the hearth. I awkwardly jumped up onto the sofa and lay beside Purza. For a while we slept, enveloped by the warmth and the festivity going on all around.

Odin woke us. "I think I've found something," he said. "Come look."

Purza and I jumped down from the sofa and followed him over to the nearest wall. "Look around. Does anything seem different to you?"

I did as he bid, looking up, down, and around. Purza did the same. I noticed nothing out of the ordinary. I twitched my whiskers in a flash of exasperation. "What is going on?"

Sensing my increasing irritation, Odin continued. "Look along the floorboards all along the walls. Everything has been cleared away from them. It's like this all around the entire room."

I looked, and since it had been pointed out to me, I saw what he was talking about. I started to walk. As I went around the room, the realization of what was happening swept over me. Not a single thing lay along the circular path. When I was finished, I turned to look at my friends. I stared at them through wide eyes, knowing what was going to happen.

"Tomorrow is Christmas. Everyone in the family will be in this room unwrapping the gifts under the tree," said Odin.

I nodded. "The Time Swiper plans to do to our family what he did to us. He plans to take away their day of happiness. He will steal it and our family will never be able to get it back."

Chapter 18

Despondently, I looked out of the window. It was my favorite one. The glass bowed outward, giving me the perfect place to sit. Odin would often join me, and together we would enjoy the sun's rays. Today, the world outside was covered under a thin blanket of white stuff the children excitedly called snow. It shimmered where the sunlight touched it, sparkling like thousands of tiny gems.

Gems that the gray gnome wouldn't hesitate to steal if he could.

My thoughts having turned sour, I turned away from the beautiful world outside and lay my head on my paws. Dad approached, and in an uncharacteristic show of affection, he smoothed his big hand over the top of my head, between my shoulders, and over my back. He then swept his hand over my distended sides, his expression pensive. I gazed up at him lovingly, happy for his rare caress. It was moments like these that told me that, indeed, he loved me. The concerned expression reflected in his blue eyes validated it.

After Dad left, I looked out the window again, entranced. The beauty was captivating. The branches of the trees, the ground, the roofs of the nearby houses… all wore the shimmering blanket of tiny diamonds. The decorative shrubbery around each house was no exception, down to the little men that stood sentry there. Peeking out from beneath white shrouds, their crimson conical hats stood at attention, bits and parts of their blue tunics and green trousers showing through here and there. White beards blended with the snow, yet I could see where they started and ended. They were human representations of friendly gnomes. They lived outside among the flowers, shrubs, and other growing things. And they were happy.

They were happy in the beautiful sunshine.

Again, I lay my head on my paws. But I didn't look away. Instead, I took in the happy faces of the garden gnomes. I knew they weren't real; they were simple human renditions. But Purza said they existed. They weren't like the evil thing the gray gnome had become. They stole underwear, not time from the lives of other beings. And according to humans, they thrived in the outdoors, among the green growing things and under the light of the sun.

I continued to lay there in to the evening. My belly ached, and I felt a pressure at the base of my tail. It scared me, so I tried not to think about it. A feeling of helplessness hung over me. No matter how much I didn't want to relive the heartache from my other life, it looked like I was destined to do so.

Purza came. And Odin. They could not move me from my place. Only Sam's arms around me could persuade me to leave, and then, when he slept peacefully in the deepest part of the night, I left. I slunk downstairs and sat before the magnificent tree. It sparkled with lights, twinkling like the tiny pinprick lights high up in the sky that the children called stars. Ornaments hung from the branches, and at the very top was the figure of an undefinable person with wings. The wings were outspread, as though waiting for those who might need to seek shelter there.

I moved under the tree, among all the packaged gifts filled with thoughtfulness and love. I moved until I reached the window located behind it. There wasn't much place to sit, but I managed it in spite of my larger form.

There I stayed, and in the early hours of the morning I abruptly awakened. I looked beyond my hiding place behind the tree and saw Purza and Odin moving in the darkness. After slinking around for a few moments, they each found a place to hide. They didn't know I was there, otherwise they would have acknowledged my presence. I felt a moment of regret, for it was very possible they wondered where I was and were concerned about my whereabouts.

Time ticked by. Even without having spoken to my comrades, I knew what we waited for. My petulance increased with pain that gripped my belly, and for the tenth time I licked that place at the base of my tail.

And suddenly, like some kind of claxon call, I knew I'd run out of time. Whatever was going to happen, I needed it to happen NOW.

Chapter 19

I dashed from my place behind the tree. Keeping out of sight of Purza and Odin, I slunk around the periphery of the room, and when they weren't looking, I darted out into the foyer and into the kitchen. Without even the briefest pause, I then slipped down into the basement.

There was no hesitation, no moment to take in my surroundings. I scurried down the stairs and into the heart of my fear. I could sense the creature there, waiting... waiting for the perfect time to execute his plan.

But I needed him to hurry up. I had something else to do this day, and it didn't include the gray gnome.

I paused only when I reached the place where Odin and I had last seen him. For a moment there was only silence. I sat in the middle of the floor, the tip of my tail moving back and forth, my ears swiveling to take in every sound.

Before I could see him, I could sense him. Just like before, the hairs rose all over my body. The malevolence he exuded was like a living thing, breathing into the silence like a bellows that only I could hear. And then he was there standing before me. He looked like his normal self... a gray gnome with gray clothes, a gray beard, and a crumpled gray hat. The only thing that gave away the charade was the smile. It reached across his entire face and was filled with sharp teeth.

I shuddered at the sight, but kept myself collected. I narrowed my eyes and slowly raised my paw in challenge. I sensed a shift in his attention and I knew I had his interest. I also knew he was not a patient creature.

I ran.

I darted across the basement floor like my life depended on it. I weaved between old pieces of furniture, stacks of mildewed boxes, and the discarded remains of lawncare equipment, cars, and huge rolls of carpet blackened with mold. I gave that gnome the chase of my life before finally heading up the stairs. By then, I could feel his anger and indignation. How dare I defy him?

The Time Swiper

I swept through the crack in the basement door, skidding across the smooth tile of the kitchen before regaining my traction and heading towards the living room. Much to my dismay, the family had already gathered.

Ma and Dad were hunkered before the Christmas tree. The children waited patiently on the sofas, expressions of delight on their faces. I wanted to stop what I had started, but the impending damage had been done.

Left without a choice, I proceeded with my plan. A feeling of regret washed over me and I was in another place and another time. *My blond-haired boy was there, his blue eyes faded and lackluster. The shine was gone, hidden beneath days and weeks filled with pain and anguish. I lay beside his frail body, my ear pressed against his chest, listening to the slow beating of his life. It got slower, and slower, and slower. I felt his small hand settle onto my side, felt his fingers caress my fur in the most loving of touches. I swiveled my ears to hear his last words, and once they were spoken, the beating that I listened for was over.*

That boy never got to experience a place like the one I had now, at least, not while I was there. Once, he may have, before sickness consumed his life and the lives all those around him. But now, in this moment of clarity, I believe I had been his shining star in the sky, his ray of sunlight that cast away the darkness that had begun to overtake his body and the minds of everyone around him who mourned his passing.

I careened into the living room, past Odin's hiding place and onto the path the Time Swiper had created. I sped along the wall, but suddenly found myself flagging. Pain blossomed from deep inside me, a pain that could no longer be denied. I looked behind me, saw the gray gnome coming swiftly with supernatural speed.

I closed my eyes tightly shut and thought of the boy who was gone. I thought of all he would no longer get to experience in life, the Christmases he would miss. I thought of the boy I had now, and how maybe, just maybe, I could save this one Christmas for him, just like I wished I could have saved one for the boy who was lost.

With some hidden reserve I didn't realize lay within me, I sprinted forward. I don't think I'd ever run so fast. I sped towards the Christmas tree with the beautiful winged person on top, and once there, I dove between the branches. I swiftly climbed the trunk, and as I reached the top, the gnome was at the window. I didn't hesitate.

I vaulted from the top of that tree, right from where the winged person sat. It was like I had my own wings as I soared through the air and landed on the curtain rod. The thing collapsed under my weight and I landed onto the floor amid a mess of cloth and tree lights that had been caught up in the fall.

Once free, I was able to look at what I had wrought. Beautiful sunshine shone through a window now devoid of the curtain, and glancing around, I saw what I was looking for. I became still when I saw him, an ethereal feeling flooding over me.

The gray gnome was no longer an animated creature. Instead, standing at my side was a thing of stone. It was perfect in every detail, down to the creases in his clothing and the crumpling of his conical hat.

Chapter 20

"Mrow," I said plaintively.

Dad tiptoed around the mess and picked me up. He deposited me into Sam's arms, whereupon I spoke again. "Mrow."

In spite of the mess that had been made, Ma and Dad handed out all the gifts from under the tree. When they reached the stone gnome, they gave one another a questioning glance.

"Oh wow!" gushed Arianna. "That is the coolest garden gnome ever!"

Alex was quickly out of his seat. "Let me see. Let me see." He came to stand beside his sister and nodded, a grin on his face. "Yeah, I like that gnome."

Arianna clasped her hands in front of her. "Can I paint him?" She saw the looks of uncertainty on Ma and Dad's faces and said, "Pleeeaaase?"

"Well, I suppose so," said Ma.

"He looks a bit creepy without some kinda color," said Dad. "So, yeah, give him a freshening up."

Arianna strode forward, and without hesitation, picked up the gray gnome that had been such a cause of worry over the past several days. "I'm going to make him look great!" she said. "Then, I going to put him outside to display him just like all our neighbors do with theirs."

The irony of this struck me as waves of discomfort rippled through my belly. I squirmed out of Sam's grasp and jumped down from the couch. I then retired upstairs, and without much thought, went to my boy's bedroom. I leaped atop his bed, and after sniffing around for a bit, and digging around at the blankets to make some semblance of the nest Sam had made for me after my fall from the bookcase, I lay down.

"Mrroww." Pain rippled across my belly, and I began to pant. I got up from my place, wandered around the bed for a minute, then lay back down. I remembered this from before, and my unease spiked. Fear teased at the corners of my mind, a greater fear than the one I had faced with the gray gnome.

This fear didn't have to do with my life. It had to do with the lives of tiny innocent beings that would rely on me to protect them from all harm.

The pain became greater and a pressure built at the base of my tail. "Mrrowww." The pressure continued to build and I pushed against it. I pushed, and pushed, and pushed some more.

And then something slipped free. I instantly began to lick at the small form enveloped by a thin, slick covering. I licked and licked, and when it broke, I tore it away. The thing within wriggled, and its tiny mouth opened as though it wanted to cry out.

"Freya?"

The sound of my name startled me and I looked towards the doorway. Odin stood there. His eye was wide. He could smell that something was happening, but from that distance, was unable to see. I gave a welcoming trill and he slowly approached the bed. He leaped atop it, and once seeing the tiny thing laying there beside me, he stopped.

The father looked at his offspring for the first time. An expression of wonder reflected in his one golden eye. He then slowly inched forward until he was beside me. He sniffed at the tiny thing, then nudged it to move it closer to my belly. Once again, the tiny mouth opened, and this time, the tiniest cry I'd ever heard emerged.

Odin curled up behind me as the pain started anew. I cried out as the door to the bedroom was suddenly flung open wide. Sam stood there at the entry, and when he saw what was happening, his brown eyes lit up so bright they were brighter than the lights on the Christmas tree downstairs.

"Ma! Come quick! You gotta see what Freya is doing in the middle of my bed!"

Chapter 21

Finally, I could rest. I had been moved from Sam's bed and instead placed in the closet. The pillow beneath me was new and soft to lay upon. Five wriggling bodies snuggled close to my belly, each one seeking comfort. They latched onto my teats and began to nurse, all but the smallest one. He needed help. I urged him to try and get close, but he was so small, and much weaker than the others.

But Ma was there. She took the baby and moved him close, parting my fur so that he could find his own spot among his brothers and sisters. She then crooned softly, soothingly, and I closed my eyes. I was so tired.

Dad came over and sat down beside Ma. He shook his head. "I thought she had been spayed."

Ma nodded. "I thought so too. I called the shelter and told them what happened. They looked into their records and found that they made a mistake. Somehow, Freya slipped through the cracks. She wasn't spayed before coming home with us."

"This explains so much," said Dad.

Ma only nodded sadly. "I just feel so bad about cutting down on her food."

Dad put a comforting hand on her shoulder. "It's alright. Just give her a bit extra now. She will appreciate and love you for it."

"I am worried about the runt of the litter." She pointed out my littlest kitten.

Dad rubbed Ma's shoulder. "With a bit of extra love and care, he will be just fine."

Several days later found me in the same place. The babies were all still there, and they were a constant wonder. They were a memory of the ones I had once lost. But now, instead of feeling pain and loss, I felt happiness and hope. Odin stayed with me most of the time, and when he wasn't there, Purza came to keep me company. She loved the babies and made certain they all stayed as close to me as possible.

The Time Swiper

It was a special day when the princess of the fairies came to visit. Maeve arrived in a sprinkling of dust from her gossamer wings. Her beautiful smile was the first thing I noticed, but after that, I saw some differences. No longer was she the twelve-year-old girl. Somehow, she had grown older. She was taller, and her face was a bit more refined. Her dress was a deeper color of green, and her hair was pulled back from her face with a comb encrusted with sparkling gems.

I thought to ask her about these differences, but there was no time before she was kneeling down before me. Her smile widened and it was like a special light shown upon me. I could see the pride reflected in her blue eyes, and it was so strong, I could feel it. That pride shifted to joy when she saw my babies. She took note of the youngest one. He was all black, and much smaller than the rest. She slowly reached out to him, and with the tip of her finger, she touched him on the center of his forehead. "To you I give fairy blessing," she whispered.

And then she was gone.

Hours later, after I had awakened from a nap, I looked upon my kittens. My gaze was captured by my youngest son; somehow, he had gotten to his feeding place before all the rest. I marveled at his tenacity, but more than that, I was taken aback by something different about him.

The fur upon his head where the princess of the fairies had touched him had turned white.

It wasn't long after that the children came home from school. Ma was in Sam's room folding laundry, and she turned and smiled when everyone came into the room. It was the first thing they had all started to do when they arrived home; they came to see me and my babies. They all made certain to not make any sudden movements, and they spoke in hushed tones. I allowed to them to pet the kittens. I loved seeing the expressions of adoration on each of their faces as they did so.

I especially loved looking at Arianna. She was doing so much better now that the gray gnome was gone. She was getting all of her work done, she was sleeping better, and she was eating again.

Most of all, she was happy.

The End

Glossary

abruptly (adv) - without warning; suddenly or unexpectedly

absurdity (adj) - utterly or obviously senseless, illogical, or untrue; laughably foolish or false

abuzz (adj) - full or live with activity

acclimate (v) - to accustom or become accustomed to a new climate or environment; adapt

acquiescence (n) - agreement or consent by silence or without objection; compliance

adjacent (adj) - lying near or close; adjoining

adversary (n) - a person, group, or force that opposes or attacks; opponent, enemy, foe

aghast (adj) - struck with overwhelming shock, amazement, or horror

agile (adj) - quick and well-coordinated in movement

amid (prep) - in the middle of; surrounded by

amiss (adj) - not quite right; inappropriate or out of place

apace (adv) - swiftly; quickly

astound (v) - shock or great surprise

atrocity (n) - a highly unpleasant or distasteful object or deed

avid (adj) - having or showing a keen interest in or enthusiasm for something

bask (v) - to revel in and make the most of something pleasing

bellows (n) - a device with an air bag that emits a stream of air when squeezed together with two handles

berth (n) - to give ample space while passing something

brunt (n) - the worst part or chief impact of a specified thing

captivate (v) - to attract and hold the interest and attention of; to charm

The Time Swiper

cast (v) - to cause (light or shadow) to appear on a surface

cease (v) - to bring or come to an end; to stop

charade (n) - an absurd pretense intended to create a pleasant or respectable appearance

claxon (n) - a kind of loud horn

cloying (adj) - excessively sweet, rich, or sentimental, especially to a disgusting or sickening degree

commonplace (adj) - not unusual; ordinary

compel (v) - to force or oblige someone to do something

concoct (v) - to create or devise (a story or a plan)

corrupt (adj) - a state of being in which a person has become less pure; lacking integrity

crave (v) - to feel a powerful desire for something

croon (v) - to speak, hum or sing in a soft, low voice

decrepit (adj) - worn out or ruined because of age or neglect denizen (n) - an inhabitant or occupant of a particular place

despondent (adj) - in low spirits from loss of hope or courage

dilapidated (adj) - (of a building or object) in a state of disrepair or ruin as a result of age or neglect

disgruntled (adj) - angry or dissatisfied

dismay (n) - consternation or distress, typically caused by something unexpected

distort (v) - to pull or twist out of shape

divert (v) - to draw (the attention) of someone from something

dominate (v) - (of something large or high) to have a commanding position

eerie (adj) - strange and often frightening; weird

elusive (adj) - difficult to find or catch

emanate (v) - to flow out from a source of origin; to come forth

The Time Swiper

endeavor (v) - to try hard to achieve a task

ensconce (v) - to settle securely or snugly

entranced (v) - to fill (someone) with wonder and delight, holding their entire attention

epitome (n) - a person or thing that is a perfect example of a particular quality or type

ethereal (adj) - extremely delicate and light in a way that seems too perfect for this world

execute (v) - to carry out or put into effect (a plan, order, or course of action)

exude (v) - (of a person) display (an emotion or quality) strongly and openly

fatigue (n) - extreme tiredness resulting from mental or physical exertion or illness

flabbergasted (adj) - greatly surprised or astonished

foreboding (n) - fearful apprehension; a feeling that something bad will happen

forlorn (adj) - pitifully sad and abandoned or lonely

foyer (n) - an entrance hall in a house or apartment

fraught (adj) - (of a situation or course of action) filled with or likely to result in (something undesirable)

garment (n) - an item of clothing

gauge (verb) - to estimate the magnitude, amount, or volume of

grimace (n) - an ugly, twisted facial expression, typically expressing disgust, pain, or wry amusement

haphazard (adj) - lacking any obvious principle or organization

haze (n) - an aggregation in the atmosphere of very fine suspended particles, giving the air an opalescent appearance that subdues colors

hearth (n) - the floor of a fireplace

hurtle (v) - to move or cause to move at great speed, typically in a wildly uncontrolled manner

immune (adj) - not affected or influenced by something

impending (adj) - about to happen; imminent

indignation (n) - anger or annoyance provoked by what is perceived as unfair treatment

infested (v) - the presence of something in large numbers, typically so as to cause disease, harm, or damage

inquiring (adj) - (of a look or expression) suggesting that information is sought

ire (n) - anger

irony (n) - a state of affairs or an event that seems contrary to what one expects and is often amusing as a result

lackluster (adj) - lacking in vitality, force or conviction; dull

lethargy (n) - a lack of energy; listless; apathetic

lithe (adj) - (especially of a person's body) thin, supple, and graceful

loiter (v) - to stand or wait around idly without apparent purpose lurch (v) - to make abrupt, unsteady, uncontrolled movement; stagger

lurking (adj) - lingering and persistent, though sometimes dimly perceived

luxuriate (v) - to enjoy oneself without stint; revel; take self-indulgent delight

macabre (adj) - disturbing or horrifying because of involvement with or depiction of injury and death

mange (n) - any of various skin diseases caused by parasitic mites, affecting animals and characterized by hair loss and scabby eruptions

mantle (n) - a shelf above the fireplace

mildew (n) - a thin whitish coating consisting of minute fungus, growing in damp places on material such as paper or leather

mottled (adj) - spotted or blotched in coloring

mournful (adj) - feeling or expressing sorrow or grief

musty (adj) - having a stale, moldy, or damp smell or flavor

myriad (n) - a countless or extremely great number

nonchalant (adj) - coolly unconcerned, indifferent, or unexcited; casual

nuisance (n) - an obnoxious or annoying person, thing, condition, pr practice

obscure (v) - to keep from being seen; conceal

offspring (n) - the young of a person or animal

olfactory (adj) - relating to the sense of smell

ominous (adj) - giving the impression that something bad or unpleasant is going to happen

oppressive (adj) - causing discomfort by being excessive, intense, or elaborate

palpable (adj) - capable of being touched or felt; tangible

peridot (n) - a green transparent variety of olivine, used as a gem perplex (v) - to be puzzled or bewildered over what is not understood or certain

petulant (adj) - moved to or showing sudden, impatient irritation, especially after some trifling annoyance

piercing (adj) - appearing to gaze deeply or penetratingly into something

piqued (adj) - (of interest or curiosity) excited or aroused

piteous (adj) - evoking or deserving pity; pathetic

preen (v) - to congratulate or pride oneself

provoke (v) - to stir up, arouse, or call forth feelings, desire or activity

purposefully (adv) - in a determined or resolute way

puzzlement (n) - a feeling of confusion through lack of understanding

quagmire (n) - a feeling or situation from which extrication is very difficult ramification (n) - a consequence of an action or event, especially when complex or unwelcome

rationale (n) - a set of reasons or a logical basis for a course of action or a particular belief

rattled (v) - to cause nervousness, worry, or irritation

rejuvenate (v) - give new energy or vigor to; revitalize

relevance (n) - the quality or state of being closely connected or appropriate

rendition (n) - an interpretation of a situation; a visual representation or reproduction

reserve (n) - a supply of a commodity not needed for immediate use but available if required

rictus (n) - a fixed grimace or grin

sanctuary (n) - a place of refuge or safety

saunter (v) - to walk in a slow, relaxed manner without any hurry or effort

savory (adj) - having an appetizing taste or smell

scale (v) - to climb up or over something high and steep

seeped (v) - (of a liquid) flow or leak slowly through a small hole or porous material

semblance (n) - resemblance; similarity

sentinel (n) - a soldier or guard whose job is to stand and keep watch

sinister (adj) - giving the impression that something harmful or evil is happening or will happen

spay (v) - to sterilize a female animal by removing the ovaries

speculative (adj) - engaged in, expressing, or based on conjecture rather than knowledge

stance (n) - the position or bearing of the body while standing, especially in specific activities such a sports

strewn (adj) - untidily scattered

subside (v) - to become less intense, violent, or severe

surveillance (n) - close observation, especially of a person under suspect

surveying (v) - to examine an area of features so as to construct a map, plan, or description

suspend (v) - to hang, usually with an attachment to something above

teat (n) - the nipple of the mammary gland of a female mammal from which milk is sucked by the young

tenacity (n) - the quality or fact of being very determined; determination

tend (v) - to care or look after; give one's attention to

tenfold (adj) - ten times as great or numerous

traction (n) - the adhesive friction of a body on some surface

tuft (n) - a cluster of small, usually soft and flexible parts, as feathers or hairs, attached or fixed closely together at a base and loose at the upper ends

tom (n) - the male of various animals, especially a turkey or domestic cat

uncharacteristic (adj) - not typical of a person or thing

vacate (v) - to leave a place or give up a position

validate (v) - to demonstrate or support the truth or value of

vault (v) - to leap or jump over while supporting or propelling oneself with one or both hands

velvet (n) - a closely woven fabric of silk, cotton or nylon that feels very soft on one side

vivid (adj) - intensely bright or deep color

waft (v) - to pass gently through the air

wrought (v) - to bring about; produce as a result

Afterward

Hands Across America was a public fundraising event held on Sunday, May 25th, 1986 when between 5 to 6.5 million people held hands for 15 minutes in an attempt to form a continuous human chain across 48 neighboring states from east to west coast in the United States. Many participants donated $10 each to reserve their place in line. The proceeds were donated to local charities to fight hunger and homelessness and help those in poverty. The event raised about $15 million for charities after operating expenses.

Not only is May a power month (yay May!), but every year (365 calendar days), the same number of companion animals (6.5 million) arrive at one of the community animal shelters nationwide. One of the largest challenges that face animal welfare organizations today is the sheer number of animals in need of assistance.

Although animals enter shelters for a variety of reasons, the majority of shelter populations are comprised of strays, rescues, and surrenders. Stray animals are often found on the streets and brought in by Good Samaritans or local law authorities. Unchecked stray populations tend to grow in areas without affordable spay/neuter facilities. About twice as many animals enter shelters as strays compared to the number that are relinquished by their owners. That means, that like Freya in this book, pets are being put out of their homes and left to fend for themselves on the streets.

There are many reasons why people sometimes abandon their pets. It could be a lifestyle change such as the birth of a child, losing a job, getting a divorce, or a difficulty with their health. Moving is another big reason. Sometimes people move and cannot bring their dog or cat with them because the new place won't allow pets.

It is important to educate people about what they are doing when they abandon a pet. Fear, pain, and longing are all things an animal can experience, and when they are abandoned, they will often be confused about being left behind and removed from the only family they have ever known. Many of these animals won't know how to fend for themselves, and out on the streets they will experience hunger, sickness, and extreme temperatures. Sometimes they will die.

However, there are ways that we can all help abandoned pets! 1) We can volunteer at a shelter. These places are always getting new animals and need as many helpers as they can get. 2) We can donate money. These funds will help animals in need of food, blankets, and medicines. 3) We can donate goods such as food, treats, toys, and litter. 4) We can adopt a pet. There are so many animals looking for someone just like you out there. And for all you know, you have been looking for someone just like them. Pedigreed animals are often nice to have, and necessary for some people (some people have allergies and they might need a hypoallergenic dog or cat), but animals of mixed heritage are often the best! 5) We can foster a homeless pet, just like Ma does in the story. This will give an animal more time so that he/she can find a forever home.

It is my sincerest desire that you enjoy this book. As always, thank you for your time and support. Happy reading!

~Tracy

About the Author

Tracy R. Ross lives in Cincinnati, Ohio with her husband, six of their eight children, four cats, and a dog. Growing up, she always loved animals and writing, and she is happy to finally be able to combine the two in the Cat Tales book series. She also loves eating pizza, smelling the air after it rains, vacations in the mountains, meeting and talking with her readers, and, of course, petting her cats!

About the Illustrator

Miriam Chowdhury is 21 years old and lives in Cincinnati, Ohio. She is currently working part-time in retail while taking college classes in order to pursue art education. Her hobbies include drawing, photography, and taekwondo. Some of her favorite things to watch are anime and horror movies; however, she doesn't like the dark and spiders! She has a really big sweet tooth, but the things she loves most in life are spending time with friends and family, making art, and cuddling with her kitty.

Made in the USA
Columbia, SC
26 August 2023

22135831R00098